DIANA ROSS
STAR SUPREME

DIANA ROSS
STAR SUPREME

BY JAMES HASKINS

Illustrated by Jim Spence

VIKING KESTREL

VIKING KESTREL
Published by the Penguin Group
Viking Penguin Inc., 40 West 23rd Street, New York, New York 10010, U.S.A.
Penguin Books Ltd, 27 Wrights Lane, London W8 5TZ England
Penguin Books Australia Ltd, Ringwood, Victoria, Australia
Penguin Books Canada Ltd, 2801 John Street, Markham, Ontario, Canada L3R 1B4
Penguin Books (N.Z.) Ltd, 182-190 Wairau Road, Auckland 10, New Zealand

Penguin Books Ltd, Registered Offices: Harmondsworth, Middlesex, England

First published in 1985 by Viking Penguin Inc.
Published simultaneously in Canada
Text copyright © James Haskins , 1985
Illustrations copyright © Jim Spence, 1985
All rights reserved

WOMEN OF OUR TIME® is a registered trademark of Viking Penguin Inc.

Library of Congress Cataloging in Publication Data
Haskins, James Diana Ross: star supreme. (Women of our time)
Summary: A biography emphasizing the early years of Diana Ross, who overcame
poverty and discrimination to become a famous singer.
1. Ross, Diana, 1944– —Juvenile literature. 2. Singers—United States—
Biography—Juvenile literature. [1. Ross, Diana, 1944– . 2. Singers. 3. Afro-
Americans—Biography.] I. Spence, Jim, ill. II. Title III. Series.
ML3930.R67H38 1985 784.5'5'00924[B] [92] 84-21897
ISBN 0-670-80549-1

Printed in the United States of America by The Book Press, Brattleboro, Vermont
Set in Garamond #3
5 7 9 10 8 6 4

CONTENTS

DIANA ROSS
STAR SUPREME

1

A Need for Love

On July 21, 1983, Diana Ross gave a free concert in
New York City's Central Park. Three hundred and
fifty thousand people came to hear her sing! Most of
them were teenagers. They streamed out of the sub-
way stations and off the buses. They filled the streets
on either side of the great green rectangle in the middle of Manhattan. Diana got excited just watching
them all arrive. When she stepped out onto the huge,
open-air stage, the crowd roared with delight. Just
then, there was a rumble of thunder. Diana's bright
orange body stocking seemed to glow as the sky grew

darker. She looked up at the rain clouds, and then down at her huge audience. Then she began to sing "Ain't No Mountain High Enough."

When the rain began to come down in big, heavy drops, she still sang. The drops began to come faster. In minutes, the rain was pouring down. Thousands of people in the audience ran for cover. Diana's long bushy hair was soon plastered to her face. Her eye makeup ran down her cheeks. Still, she kept on singing. Only when lightning made it dangerous for her to go on did she stop. "I'm sorry!" she called to the backs of her fleeing fans. "Come back tomorrow night."

The following night, she gave her concert. That meant that she had to pay all the musicians and technical people a second time. But she thrilled the crowd with a wonderful show. Diana Ross is not a quitter. No matter what happens to her, she does not give up. She tries very hard never to disappoint her fans. She needs their love and will do whatever she can to keep it.

"I always wanted everybody to care about me. Love me, love me, love me, please." That's what Diana told Barbara Walters in a TV interview. She thinks that being a middle child might have something to do with that need.

Diana was the second of six children in her family. First came her older sister, Barbara. Diana, born March

26, 1944, came next. Her mother named her Diane, but somehow the name went down on the birth certificate as Diana. She is still Diane to her family. After Diana came three boys and another girl. They all lived in a small apartment on the third floor of an old apartment house in the northern part of Detroit, Michigan. All the children slept together in one bedroom. In the summer, that could be pretty uncomfortable. The one window was opened as wide as it could be. Trouble was, this invited the "chinch bugs" to come in. Diana remembers her mother putting a kerosene lamp on the dresser to keep the bugs away. In the winter, the children were glad for the extra warmth of each other's bodies, for the old house was drafty and cold.

They lived in a black neighborhood. Outsiders would have called it a ghetto. Diana would not. "I would never say the ghetto, because I'm from that neighborhood, that's my home. That's not a ghetto to me. That's a ghetto to people from the outside. It's a ghetto to people who are trying to put a circle around things." As a child, Diana knew only her own neighborhood. She didn't know there were other kinds of neighborhoods. She thought everybody lived the way they did. She didn't even know she was poor.

Diana's father, Fred, worked at a brass factory. Her mother, Ernestine, stayed home and took care of the children. As each new baby arrived, little Diana felt

5

more and more need for attention. It was very hard to get attention with all those babies around. She wished she was the oldest, like Barbara. To Diana, that made Barbara *somebody*. The other children were somebodies because they were the babies. Diana did not feel that she fit in. Sometimes she got so disgusted that she would take a long, long walk. She probably hoped that her mother would miss her and come looking for her. After a while, she would find herself on a strange street and get a little bit scared. She would turn and go back home. It was sort of like pretending to run away. Her mother probably knew exactly what she was doing, and let her go because it was good for Diana to be independent. But Diana understood only that no one had come to look for her.

Diana wished she could be like her older sister Barbara. Barbara was very quiet and well behaved and she read all the time. Diana had too much energy to stay very long in one place. She would rather be outside playing than inside reading. Since she could not be like her sister, she decided to be very *un*like her sister. Maybe that would get her some attention. She was a tomboy and preferred climbing fences and raiding apple trees with the neighborhood boys to reading or playing with dolls. She loved to run, and she could beat most of the boys in races.

She was not afraid of getting into fights with kids

twice her age. It was her job to watch her younger brothers and sister when they were outside playing, and she took that job very seriously. Anyone who bothered the little ones had Diana to answer to. She didn't always win the fights she got into. But in her opinion she didn't lose either. Whenever anyone knocked her down, she'd scream, "I may be down, but I ain't down!" They always knew what she meant.

For all her tomboy qualities, Diana could be very feminine. She loved pretty dresses and pretty shoes. She loved the quiet times when her mother would stop working and take a rest. She would put some Billie Holiday records on the record player and sing along with them. Diana would sing along with them, too. Both her mother and father liked to sing and were members of the choir at Olivet Baptist Church. They were pleased that Diana had a good voice. When company came, Diana's parents would often ask her to sing for them. Diana loved the attention. After a while, whenever she heard that company was coming, she would put on her prettiest dress and be all ready to perform. She would hang around just waiting to be asked.

She was only about six years old when she learned that her singing could get her things that she wanted. She very much wanted a pair of shiny black patent leather shoes, and her father felt sorry that he did not

have the money to buy them for her. Mr. Ross always made Christmas a wonderful time, with lots of presents. But in between Christmases, his children did not often get special things. One evening, company came. Diana sang and danced for them, and the people were delighted. Suddenly, her father had an idea. He passed his hat around, and the people put money in it. He collected enough money to buy Diana her patent leather shoes. Diana probably started dreaming of new dresses and all sorts of other things. But her father never passed the hat again. He was a proud man and did not want to make a habit of passing the hat.

By the time she entered elementary school, Diana was an outgoing girl who had no trouble making friends. Many of her classmates in the all-black school were children from the neighborhood. She was bright and quick to learn. But what she liked most about going to school was playing sports. She loved to run races. She loved to swim in the school's pool and felt lucky to go to the only elementary school in the city that had a pool. She was so skinny that her teachers worried about her health. But she was not frail. Her wiry little legs and arms were all muscle. She just never sat still long enough to gain any weight. She used up her energy by running, jumping, swimming, and getting into fights.

She also liked music period at school. She would

sing and dance whenever she got the chance and was always one of the performers at school assemblies. She never once remembers being nervous about getting up on a stage and singing in front of a lot of people. She joined the junior choir at church and remembers that the first time she sang a solo she was quite young, but not a bit afraid.

The scariest thing Diana remembers about her childhood was the time when her mother got sick and the family had to split up for a while. Mrs. Ross had tuberculosis and had to go to a special hospital in Holland, Michigan. Mr. Ross was working a full shift at American Brass and doing side jobs as a mechanic. He could not take care of six children. So, all the children were sent to live with Mrs. Ross's parents until she got well.

Mrs. Ross's parents lived in Bessemer, Alabama. The Reverend William Moton was pastor of Alabama Bessemer Baptist Church. He and his wife welcomed their six grandchildren. They had raised twice that many children of their own.

Diana was around nine when she and her sisters and brothers went to live with their grandparents. She remembers missing her parents. But with all her brothers and sisters there, she was not really lonely. Her grandparents' lives centered around the church and so, of course, did the children's. They went to church services and Sunday school and choir practice. There was a lot of singing at the church services. Diana loved the rich gospel music that filled the church each Sunday.

Diana had to get used to a new school and make new friends. But she didn't find that hard. The hardest thing, besides missing her parents, was understanding why there was so much segregation in Bessemer, Alabama.

In Alabama, in the mid-1950s, there were separate drinking fountains for blacks and whites. There were separate waiting rooms in the bus stations. On the buses, black people had to pay at the front, then go around to the back door to get on. They could only sit in the back, and if the seats for the whites up front got filled up, the blacks had to give up their seats. Some restaurants would serve blacks, but only through the back door. Blacks could only enter white stores from the back. They could not try on shoes before they bought them.

Diana was not affected by these things all the time. Her grandparents lived in a black neighborhood. The members of their church were black. Diana and her brothers and sisters attended a black school. But she remembers having to go in back doors and having to drink from certain water fountains and only being able to go to certain places to eat. She didn't understand why she had to do these things. Her grandparents didn't really explain why, and so she was left to wonder, Why do we have to use the back door? What is wrong with us? She began to think there must be something wrong with being black.

After about a year, Diana's mother was well enough to return home. The children left Bessemer and went back to Detroit. There they quickly took up their old lives. Many of their friends had relatives in the South and spent summers there. No one thought anything of the fact that the Ross children had been in Alabama for a year.

Diana wanted to talk about segregation in the South, but no one else wanted to. After a time, she thought of her experiences with segregation as a bad dream. Even so, the memory of it did not go away. Maybe this is another reason that she had such a great need to be loved.

2

Singing in the Streets

One of the things Diana had missed about her Detroit neighborhood was the variety of music in it. Her grandparents had frowned on pop music. They only liked gospel. And the kids in Bessemer did not sit outside and play their radios like the kids did in Detroit. "We used to sit outside on the stoop and sing. We even used to put our radios and record players outside. Kids always wanted to listen to music outside because that's where they hung out with their friends. It just wasn't an inside thing to do." Besides, most of them lived in apartments so small that they wanted to be outside whenever they could.

Out on the stoop, Diana would sing by herself or harmonize with her friends. They sang along to all kinds of music. But they especially liked the new rock and roll. And they really liked the songs sung by groups. Perhaps that was because they could sing along with the harmony. They could also dream of being in a singing group one day.

This was not just a dream in Diana's north Detroit neighborhood. Right down the street lived William "Smokey" Robinson, who was four years older than Diana. He and four friends had a singing group called the Miracles. They were very popular in the area and sometimes got a chance to sing at record hops. Diana was proud to live near Smokey. His niece, Sharon, was one of her best friends, and Diana spent as much time as she could at Sharon's house. She was always hoping to see Smokey.

While Diana was attending Dwyer Junior High School, Smokey Robinson and the Miracles became even bigger celebrities. They were the first group signed by a new black record company in Detroit. Hitsville USA was started by a young record-store owner and songwriter named Berry Gordy. He did not have to look far for talent. Detroit's black neighborhoods were full of young singers and musicians. Soon he had signed contracts with groups like the Marvellettes and individuals like Mary Wells and Little Stevie Wonder.

Half the black teenagers in Detroit now dreamed of being discovered by Berry Gordy. Diana was among them. All she could think about was singing. Her father was not happy about that. He wanted her to do something important, and he did not consider singing important. Although Diana managed to get B+ grades, she did not like to study. When she did have to be inside, she much preferred to watch TV.

The TV had been her father's present to the whole family one Christmas. Diana immediately rushed out and invited the whole neighborhood in to see it. She loved that television. She would watch anything that came on. But her favorite shows were musical variety shows. She liked to watch the lady singers in their beautiful evening gowns. Trouble was, just about all the people she saw on TV were white. She wondered why they wouldn't let any black people be on TV. Once again, she wondered if there was something wrong with being black. Television also showed Diana that her family must be poor after all. She knew they could not afford the clothes and cars and other things that all the white people on TV seemed to have.

By the time Diana was graduated from junior high school, things were looking up for the Ross family. They moved to a bigger apartment. It was in a low-income housing project on the east side of Detroit called the Brewster-Douglass Projects. Diana understood that the Brewster-Douglass Projects were a place where "you had to be poor just to get in," but she liked having a little more space, no matter where it was.

Diana did not attend a local high school. Her B+ average in junior high made it possible for her to go to Cass Technical High School, one of the best high schools in the city. There, Diana took courses in dress design, sewing, costume illustration, and cosmetology. She had listened to her father and tried to concentrate on a practical career. She wanted to be a model or a fashion designer. She went to charm school at Hudson's department store downtown on Saturdays.

Diana auditioned for a part in a Cass Tech musical. She sang "Ebb Tide," a slow ballad. The music teacher said she had a pretty good voice, but it was not what he was looking for. She took that to mean that he really didn't think she was good at all. She did not realize that he was looking for the kind of loud, strong voice that singers in stage musicals must have. She should have chosen a different song to sing. But Diana did not think about that.

At Cass Tech, for the first time in her life, really, Diana felt unsure of herself. Her fellow students came from all over the city and even from the suburbs of Detroit. The majority of them were white. It was the first time that Diana had come into close contact with white kids. She was not sure how to act around them. She was very self-conscious of her clothes, her hair, of how skinny she was. The outgoing, confident Diana seemed to disappear the minute she walked through the school doors.

But the Diana who would fight kids twice her size when she was a little girl was still there. She didn't say, "I may be down, but I ain't down" any more. But she still believed it. She was still determined to be *somebody*. She would show that music teacher and everyone else. She was just more quiet about it.

Diana wrote notes to herself. She wrote her goals on a piece of paper and looked at it every day. At that time her biggest dream was to be a famous model. She practiced in front of the mirror.

She did make new friends outside of school. Mary Wilson and Florence Ballard also lived in the Brewster-Douglass Projects, although she did not meet them there. She met them when she joined the choir in the local Baptist church. She and Mary became good friends. Diana's mother had bought her a sewing machine, and she and Mary designed and made their own clothes. They studied fashion magazines. They tried out different kinds of makeup and styled each other's hair. Diana told Mary about her dreams for the future, something she did not share with many people.

Diana and Mary also shared a love of singing. In

17

fact, Mary was part of a group called the Primettes. They were a sister group to the Primes, a group of boys who sang at record hops and parties. Florence Ballard was also a Primette, and there were two other girls in the group. Diana longed to be in the Primettes. But the other girls did not think there should be more Primettes than Primes.

Then, one of the girls dropped out. Diana got her

chance. But first she had to prove that she was good enough. The Primettes were not going to let her into their group without an audition. So one evening they went out onto the grounds of the Brewster-Douglass Projects and sang for the neighborhood. People gathered around and clapped their hands. Someone passed around a hat. The girls got $3.00. Diana became a full-fledged Primette.

Right away, Diana started dreaming about being part of a beautiful and famous singing group. All she could think about was singing. In her excitement, she forgot that her father thought singing all day was a waste of time. He thought even less of the idea that the Primettes sang at night—at record hops and parties. In fact, he said that Diana could not go.

Diana loved her parents and did not want to disobey her father. But she would not give up her membership in the group. She lied about where she was going at night. Even after her father punished her for staying out late, she continued to go with the Primettes every time they had a chance to sing. After a while, her father gave in.

Florence Ballard had an even harder time than Diana did. Her family did not want her to be part of a singing group. She often missed practices. And when her grades went down one marking period, she was forbidden to sing with the group any longer. When that happened,

Diana was very upset. They needed Florence's voice. Diana saw her dreams disappearing. She could not let that happen. It was she who called up Florence's family and begged them to change their minds. Like Diana's father, they gave in.

Mary Wilson was the lead singer in the Primettes. Diana was a backup singer, along with Florence and Barbara Martin. But Diana soon became its leader in other ways. She was the one who designed and sewed their matching outfits. The first was black and gold. They wore strings of fake gold beads from the dime store. Another outfit was a balloon-skirted dress in a bright orange-flowered print, with bright orange shoes decorated with a big flower on the front. Diana was the one who decided they should audition for Hitsville. She got in touch with Smokey Robinson from her old neighborhood. She asked him to listen to the Primettes, and he did. He even got them an audition.

All four girls were nervous when they sang for Berry Gordy, the president of Hitsville. They had carefully rehearsed their song and the way they would move when they sang. Diana had made new matching outfits for them all. When they finished singing, they thought they had done well. Berry Gordy agreed. But there was just no way he was going to offer them a contract. Hitsville performers had to be able to go on tour, and the Primettes were still in high school. He

told them to come back after they graduated.

The girls were so disappointed. But Diana refused to give up. She pestered the people at Hitsville until at last Gordy said they could sing backup in the recording studio. They backed up Marvin Gaye, Mary Wells, Marv Johnson, Martha Reeves and the Vandellas, Junior Walker and the All-Stars. They received $2.50 apiece for each song. Berry Gordy paid them personally. Every time she got a chance, Diana reminded him that they wanted to make records of their own.

Being a member of the Primettes made a big difference in Diana's life. It changed her whole attitude at school. She was part of a *group*, and that was like having a big, warm coat on. Now she strode through the doors of Cass Tech every weekday morning. She said "hi" to everyone she passed. Everyone said "hi" back. They looked up to her as somebody. At the same time, she began to realize that her new popularity wasn't all because she was a Primette. Part of it was due to her own attitude. "I found out that if you think you're somebody, you *are* somebody," she said.

Diana and the Primettes continued to sing every chance they got. More often than not, they were not paid. The $2.50 Berry Gordy gave them for doing backup singing barely covered the cost of carfare to and from the Hitsville studio. To earn extra money,

Diana got a job at Hudson's department store.

Most of the people who worked at Hudson's were white. Even the people who picked up the dirty dishes in the store cafeteria where white—until Diana was hired. She was the first black "bus girl" at Hudson's. People went to the basement cafeteria just to look at her. Proud Diana held her head high. "I made it a point to be beautifully groomed and to make a fine impression," she says. "Nobody would ever have anything bad to say about Diane."

All she could think about was how she looked and about singing. She spent hours dreaming about being famous. "I'm the creation of my own imagination," she has said. She means that, in her dreams, she was a star long before she really was one. She did not care about studying. Now she wishes she had paid more attention at school. Out in the show-business world, she often didn't know what people around her were talking about. Even worse for Diana was the fact that she delayed the start of her own career by not paying attention to her schoolwork. She did not graduate when Mary and Florence did. She had to take an extra semester to graduate from Cass Tech.

3

Motown at Last

Diana was graduated from Cass Tech in January 1962. She was voted Best-Dressed Girl. By this time, the fourth Primette, Barbara Martin, had dropped out of the group. It was just Mary, Florence, and Diana. As he had promised, Berry Gordy put them under contract. That is not to say that they began to record or go out on tour right away. There was a lot of work to be done first.

Berry Gordy didn't just produce records. He produced *acts*. The way his performers looked, dressed, danced, acted, and spoke was as carefully planned as the songs they sang. The girls learned how to move about gracefully on a stage. The Hitsville choreographer gave them a sideways head-over-the-shoulder stance and special hand gestures, which they did in unison. The makeup department created a glamorous "look" for them: heavy, penciled eyebrows; eyes ringed with thick black eyeliner; white lipstick; high, teased wigs. They changed their name from the Primettes to the Supremes. Earlier, Gordy had signed the male group, the Primes, to a contract. Their name was changed to the Temptations.

A lot of changes took place at Hitsville that year, 1962. It was the year when all of Gordy's hard work and careful planning began to pay off. He had five hit records that year. He also changed the name of his company. Detroit was known as Motor Town because of all the cars that were made there. Gordy shortened that to Motown. The company has been Motown ever since.

Motown was an exciting place to be, even for the office workers. But it was like heaven for Diana. She liked being around all the Motown performers who'd had hits. She watched the girls closely. She thought maybe they had some secret she could copy. She dreamed about what it would be like when the Supremes had a hit.

When the Supremes made their first recordings

Diana, not Mary, sang lead vocal. Berry Gordy decided that Diana's voice was more "commercial." Diana probably wanted to call up that Cass Tech music teacher right then and there. Gordy may have had another reason for choosing Diana to be lead singer: The lead vocalist in a Motown act was the one who spoke to the audience between numbers, and Diana proved to be best at that. She spoke well and never muffed a line. Mary Wilson was disappointed that Diana had been chosen over her, but she tried not to show it. All three girls agreed that the most important thing was for the group to succeed.

Their first two records actually reached the Top 100 on the charts. But they were surrounded by Motown acts with Top Ten records. Everyone told them not to worry. Their turn would come. In the meantime, the Supremes got to go out on tour with the other Motown acts.

It was during their first Motor Town Revue that Diana found a way to copy the other girls' acts. She studied their moves onstage and saw no harm in "borrowing" some of those moves. The other performers resented this, but Berry Gordy did not reprimand her. In fact, Diana was so energetic onstage, such a crowd-pleaser, that Gordy soon moved the Supremes to a better position in the lineup. Diana acted as if she had been born to the stage. The love she felt coming from the audience was like nothing she had ever felt before.

The Motor Town Revue played black theaters in cities across the country. Motown music wasn't really accepted by most whites yet. Partly, that was because the music business itself was quite segregated, although that situation was beginning to change.

Given the chance, though, the Motor Town Revue could have moved right into the biggest white theater at a moment's notice. Berry Gordy trained his acts to be perfectly groomed and professional. The audiences never realized that behind all the glamour up on stage was a lot of drudgery.

It was not glamorous to ride all night on a bus. It was hard work to play several shows one night in one city and then travel hundreds of miles to play several shows the next night in another city. "There was a time on that first tour that they wouldn't let us off the bus until everybody had their makeup on," Diana recalls. "It was the day of the beehive, and your hair had to stay teased up like that for days." Not only did they have to sleep on the bus most nights, they also had to sleep stiff-necked, so they wouldn't muss their hairdos. Diana loved being on stage so much that she didn't mind. But after about a year, Mary and Florence were ready to give up. Even Diana had to admit that it was hard to act like stars when they were not.

In 1963, the Motor Town Revue played the Apollo

Theatre in Harlem. For the Supremes, it was the first time, and they were very excited. The Apollo was *the* place for black performers. You couldn't call yourself an entertainer until you had played the Apollo. Apollo audiences were tough. It they didn't like you they would throw cans and bottles. The people who ran the Apollo were also tough. They paid a man to drag unpopular performers off the stage with the crook of a cane. If the master of ceremonies didn't think an act was very important, he didn't even bother to "take them off the stage" with a closing announcement.

That's what happened to the Supremes one night. The master of ceremonies was there to introduce them to the audience. But when they finished performing he was not there to say the last "Ladies and gentlemen, the Supremes." A comedian named Scoey Mitchell was due onstage next. He was waiting in the wings. When he realized that the MC wasn't anywhere around, he "took them off the stage" himself. He said, "Ladies and gentlemen, the Supremes," and the girls thought it was part of his job. They left the stage, and Mitchell did his act. The next show that night the same thing happened. The MC wasn't anywhere around when they finished their performance. Mitchell decided that he wasn't getting paid to be MC. After a few embarrassing moments, the Supremes had to walk off the stage in silence.

When Mitchell came offstage after doing his act, there was a message waiting for him: "Miss Ross wants to see you upstairs." He went up to the Supremes' dressing room. There, an angry Diana demanded to know why he hadn't been there to take them off. He explained that he wasn't the MC. Diana didn't care who he was. And that was when he decided to remind her who *she* was, or wasn't. "I tell you what, little girl," he said, "You better stop fussing with me and go and try and get yourself a hit record."

That took Diana down a peg or two. She didn't like being a nobody in the music business. She started thinking that maybe Florence and Mary had the right idea after all.

But the Supremes decided to hang on, at least a little while longer. The best writing team at Motown was writing a song for them. Brian and Eddie Holland and Lamont Dozier had written two big hits for Martha and the Vandellas. Holland-Dozier-Holland wrote "Where Did Our Love Go" for the Supremes in early 1964. They recorded it a few months later. The Supremes loved the song and had their fingers crossed. Soon after the record's release, they went on their first tour with Dick Clark. They didn't have a chance to fret about the progress of their record.

Their first tour with Dick Clark was also their first integrated tour. Clark was the MC of the popular

American Bandstand TV show, and he was a kind of pioneer in playing records by blacks and having black guest stars. He also invited black performers to be part of his "Cavalcade of Stars" road show.

While the Supremes were on that tour they learned that they had a hit record at last! One night they launched into the first few bars of "Where Did Our Love Go," and the audience clapped and cheered. The song was being played on local radio stations. From then on, everywhere they went, they got the same reaction to "Where Did Our Love Go." And by the time the tour was over and they returned to Detroit, the Supremes had a Number One hit!

"Where Did Our Love Go" was only the first in a long string of hits for the Supremes. It was followed by "Baby Love," "Stop! In the Name of Love," "Come See About Me," "Back in My Arms Again," and "I Hear a Symphony." The Supremes were the first group ever to have six hit records in a row in the space of a single year.

Scoey Mitchell was the comedian at the Apollo who had told Diana she'd better concentrate on trying to get a hit record. Now, every time he saw her, he said, "You listen good!"

4

Dream Come True

The Supremes did what no other Motown act had been able to do. They made the "crossover" to the white audience. White kids bought their records and wrote them fan letters. White kids wanted to see them in concert. That was fine with Berry Gordy. He had hoped all along to break into the white market someday. He knew that he only needed one act to do it. White people who liked the Supremes would also be willing to listen to Smokey Robinson and the Miracles, Martha and the Vandellas, and the other acts. The Supremes were the trailblazers.

In October 1965, the Supremes played a concert at Philharmonic Hall in New York. It was the first time a Motown act had ever played there. For Diana, it was a night to remember. She realized that the Diana she had imagined for so many years finally existed. Her dream had come true. "There we were, being glamorous just like in the fashion magazines . . . in yellow chiffon and flowers singing 'Baby Love' and 'Where Did Our Love Go' and getting devotion from an audience of feeling people who have a respect for the art of show business." She had the concert poster blown up really big and hung it on her wall. She explained that "it caught our dreams and aspirations and who we thought we were at the time."

That same year, they realized another of their dreams—they became rich. They felt as if they could conquer the world. They all turned twenty-one and were able to control the monies that Motown had been holding in trust for them.

For girls who had grown up poor the way Diana and Mary and Florence had, having money was the best part of their dream-come-true. The first thing they all did was to buy houses for their families. All the houses were on the same street in the northwest section of Detroit. Then, they all gave money to their parents. At least Diana tried to. Her father still did not believe that singing was a very practical career. He told her to save her money.

But Diana could not. At least not at first. For years she had dreamed of having the things she saw on TV and in Hudson's department store. She could afford to have them now, and she intended to.

Diana did not stop dreaming when her teenage dreams came true. She started dreaming other dreams. She still wrote notes to herself and looked at them every day. She wanted the Supremes to appear at nightclubs in front of adult audiences. She wanted to record songs that were "old favorites." She got what she wanted. The Supremes played the Copacabana in New York. They played Las Vegas. They recorded a whole album of Beatles songs, as well as ballads.

By this time there were few wishes of Diana's that Berry Gordy would not grant. She was clearly his favorite. He took a special interest in building up her voice, giving her tapes to study, often coaching her himself. Since just about every girl singer at Motown had a crush on Gordy, his relationship with Diana was another cause for resentment against her. Not only was she obviously special to him, but she acted as if she were special.

Meanwhile, Mary Wilson and Florence Ballard just seemed to move farther and farther into the background. Diana was the star. Gordy started escorting Diana to public events and telling Mary and Florence to attend separately. Mary and Florence lost confidence. They didn't feel like Supremes at all, just a couple of backup singers for Diana.

Mary realized that she had to start speaking up. She asked to sing lead sometimes at concerts, and she got her wish. Florence just seemed to give up. She started missing recording sessions. Sometimes she didn't even show up for concerts. She began to drink heavily. Berry Gordy often thought of firing her. But Mary and Diana would not hear of it. They could not imagine the Supremes without Florence.

Theirs was still a winning sound. Songs like "My World Is Empty Without You," "You Can't Hurry Love," "You Keep Me Hanging On," "Love is Here and Now You're Gone," and "The Happening" were big hits. They had so many gold records they ran out of wall space. Gold records are like trophies, given after records sell more than half a million copies.

But by 1967 Berry Gordy had decided that Florence Ballard's voice would no longer be part of that sound. Knowing that Diana and Mary would be furious if he fired Florence, he said he was just going to replace her "temporarily." Florence was too proud to go along with that. She quit, and Mary and Diana could not make her change her mind. A girl named Cindy Birdsong took her place.

After Florence left, Gordy changed the way the Supremes were billed. Instead of the Supremes, they

became Diana Ross and the Supremes. Diana had emerged as the star long before the name change. Reporters wanted to interview her alone. TV producers wanted her to be a guest on their shows— alone. Diana liked being singled out in this way, although she did feel a little guilty about it.

It took two more years before Diana realized that she could not do all the things she wanted to do alone and still be with the Supremes. But at last, in the middle of 1969, she told Mary and Cindy that she was going to quit the group and try a solo career. They were not surprised. They knew it was going to happen sooner or later. When the public announcement was made, there was very little reaction. The fans also seemed to have known that Diana would go out on her own.

Diana Ross and the Supremes gave their "farewell performance" at the Frontier Hotel in Las Vegas on January 14, 1970. At the end, they were all sobbing. Mary and Diana had been together for ten years. Mary wondered what the Supremes would be like without Diana. Diana wondered what she would be like without the Supremes.

5

On Her Own

The first album issued by Motown that had Diana's name on it without the Supremes was not a Diana Ross album. Instead, it was the first album by a group called the Jackson Five. They were a family of young boys from Gary, Indiana, and newly under contract with Motown.

Diana had met them in the summer of 1968 in Gary, where both she and they performed at the same event. She loved them, especially Michael, who had just turned eleven. "Michael won me over the first moment I met him," she has said. "I saw so much of myself as a child in Michael. He was performing all the time. That's the way I was. He could be my son." She told Berry Gordy that he just had to sign the Jackson Five to a contract. A few months later, he did.

Many people feel that Diana got too much credit for "discovering" the Jackson Five. Even Michael has said that no one discovered the Jackson Five but their parents. It is likely that they would have become stars anyway, with or without Motown. But Diana is the one who got Berry Gordy to really pay attention to them.

By that time, Berry Gordy's attention was on his new TV and film business. He was setting up a whole new division of Motown in Hollywood. He had bought a house out there. Diana soon moved there, too. The Jacksons were not far behind. In fact, some of the boys lived with Gordy and some lived with Diana for a while. Michael stayed with Diana for about a year and a half. It was one of the best times of his life. They went to Disneyland and had fun every day. Michael developed a crush on twenty-four-year-old Diana. He still has it to this day. For Diana, Michael became her "baby." The Jackson Five's first album, released in the fall of 1969, was called *Diana Ross Presents the Jackson Five*.

Not long afterward, Motown released Diana's first

solo album. It was called *Diana Ross*. Gordy advertised it with a huge blowup of the album cover on a one-hundred-foot-high billboard on Sunset Boulevard in Los Angeles. The picture showed Diana alone, and lonely. That is the way she felt.

A song on her first solo album seemed to be about the way she was feeling. It was called "Reach Out and Touch (Somebody's Hand)." But if she was lonely in her personal life, she had plenty of love from her fans. Her album was a hit and so were some of her first singles as a solo artist. *Billboard* magazine named her "top female singer of 1970." The biggest hit she had was "Ain't No Mountain High Enough." It became her theme song. The words were about loving someone so much that even the highest mountain could not keep her from him.

But the way Diana sang them, the words also meant something else. They meant that she wasn't going to let anything stand in the way of what she wanted. She was still the stubborn girl who used to say, "I may be down, but I ain't down." She had found it very hard to be a solo performer when she had been a Supreme for so long. Alone on a stage, she felt exposed, as if something was missing. Her solo voice sounded small and weak without the voices of Mary and Cindy. Some critics charged that she and Motown tried to cover up the weakness of her voice by making her show like a fashion show, with many changes of expensive costumes and wigs. They said she was overproduced. But audiences seemed to understand how important it was to her to perform. They wanted her to succeed, and Diana seemed to sense that. She opened her first shows as a solo with, "Good evening, and welcome to the Let's-see-if-Diana-Ross-can-make-it-on-her-own show." The audiences responded with the love she needed to have from them.

By the time "Ain't No Mountain High Enough" was released, Diana had someone she loved to sing it to. His name was Robert Silberstein, an actors' agent in Hollywood who used the name Robert Ellis. Diana met him in a men's clothing store in Hollywood. She asked if she could hold a shirt up to him to judge its size, and soon they were talking and laughing. A handsome, dark-haired man, he was a few months younger than Diana. He was also white. The fact that they were of different races did not matter to them. But they knew that it did matter to other people. They dated quietly for about a year before they decided to get married. As much as she needed love, Diana was not sure she wanted to be married—to anyone.

In January 1971, they suddenly decided to go ahead. Diana told herself that she could be married and have a career, too. When they made the public announcement, they were shocked by the reaction. A lot of people, white and black, did not like it. Diana and Bob tried not to let the opinions of other people affect their relationship, and they were largely successful. Being of different races was not the source of the problems they had. Their problems were caused by their different ideas of what marriage should be.

Berry Gordy and Motown officially supported Diana's marriage to Bob. Berry Gordy kept his private opinions to himself. He and Diana's business partnership went on as before, and Diana did not slacken her performance schedule after her marriage. That caused tension between her and her new husband. He wanted her to be home more. Then Diana became pregnant, and she worried that it was too soon after the start of her solo career. The strains on their marriage were so great during that first year that Diana and Bob actually separated for a time a few months after the wedding. They managed to keep it a secret because Diana was on the road so much that no one knew the difference. The separation was a brief one, and when Rhonda Suzanne was born, Diana forgot all her doubts. That baby was the most important thing in the world to her.

Rhonda Suzanne was only four months old when Diana began filming a movie. Motown's first film was to be about Billie Holiday, the legendary jazz singer who had died in 1959 at the age of forty-four. Diana had the starring role in *Lady Sings the Blues*.

Diana's life had been very different from Billie Holiday's. Holiday never had the strong family life that Diana had enjoyed. By age twenty-five she was very popular with jazz fans. But along the way she became addicted to heroin, and she died because of it. Her whole short life was filled with pain. But no one could sing jazz and the blues the way she could.

Diana read as much as she could about Billie Holiday. She listened to her records, over and over again.

That brought back happy memories of her childhood, when her mother would sit down and rest and the two of them would listen to Billie Holiday records. Back then, Diana had just enjoyed the music and being with her mother. Now, she listened and tried to understand how Holiday had thought and felt. When filming began, Diana was nervous about her first big acting role.

No one could help her find the hate and despair that Holiday had felt. Diana had to go inside herself to find them. She was surprised to find that they were inside her, pushed way back because she hadn't wanted to think about them. She remembered her unhappiness at not getting enough attention as a child. She remembered segregation down South and realizing that she was poor. She remembered the despair she and Mary and Florence had felt when everyone at Motown seemed to have a hit record but them.

No one could help her sing Holiday's songs. She decided not to try to imitate Holiday's voice. She sang with her own voice. But she did sing in Holiday's style, pronouncing the words the same way and using the same phrasing (dividing the melody into the same small groups of notes).

Movies were hard work, she found. She worked twelve hours a day for forty-one days. Some of the saddest and most violent scenes in the film were shot again and again. That meant that Diana had to be sad or angry for hours at a time. Every night she returned home exhausted. But she had to be up again at five the next morning. She had to be back at the studio at six A.M. Meanwhile, she learned that she was pregnant again.

Filming was completed at the end of February 1972, but the movie was not released until late October. There was a glamorous premier in New York City. But Diana could not attend. Her second baby was due too soon. Tracee Joy was born in early November.

Many movie critics did not like *Lady Sings the Blues*. But these same critics praised Diana's performance. They said she was "real." She was nominated for an Academy Award for Best Actress. She did not win, but even to be nominated is a great honor. For Diana, it was proof that she could do anything if she worked hard enough.

Diana had a lot to be proud about. She was a success as a solo singer. She was a success as an actress. She had a husband she loved and two beautiful little girls. No mountain had been high enough to keep her from getting what she wanted.

6

More of Everything

Diana was proud of her work in *Lady Sings the Blues*. She wanted to do more movies. She also wanted to do more records. In 1973 her album *Touch Me in the Morning* was released. The title song, issued as a single, reached Number One on the charts. But her favorite part of being an entertainer was performing before a live audience. To her, it was like having waves of love wash over her. She really missed it. One movie and two babies had kept her away from the concert stage for more than two years.

So, as soon as she could leave Tracee Joy, she started rehearsing a new stage show. Then she went back on the road. Diana's parents had divorced and her mother now lived with her. Her mother and a nurse took care of the children. Diana took her show to England. Back in the United States, she played Lake Tahoe, Nevada.

She missed being at home with her husband and children. But she had found out that she was bored and restless staying at home. She decided that everyone would be better off if she was doing what she really wanted to do.

After a few months, Diana was ready to go back into the recording studio. Three albums were released that year. The title song of her album *Last Time I Saw Him* was released as a single and reached the top fifteen on the charts. She also started filming another Motown movie, *Mahogany*.

Mahogany is about a poor fashion design student in Chicago who becomes a famous model *and* fashion designer. Not only did Diana get to star as Mahogany, she also got to design the clothes that Mahogany designed in the film. In a way, the film gave her a chance to live out the smaller dreams she'd had in high school. She had studied fashion design. She had gone to charm school and wanted to be a model.

Not long after she finished filming *Mahogany*, Diana learned that she was pregnant a third time. The news had a strong effect on her. Somehow, the idea of having *three* children made her feel that she could not have a career and be a good mother, too. Ever since

her marriage, she had seesawed back and forth between being a wife and mother who stayed at home and being a glamorous entertainer. She could not seem to combine both successfully, so she decided to stop trying. She cancelled all her appearances. Chudney Lane Silberstein was born November 11, 1975.

Mahogany premiered about a month later. Movie critics did not think much of it. They called it "glossy" and "unrealistic." Diana got no special praise for her acting. The movie's poor reception bothered Diana a lot. If she had been working, she would have kept herself busy enough to have little time to worry about it. But she was at home, with lots of time on her hands. She had many empty hours to fill worrying that she had quit at the wrong time, that she should have quit when she was on top.

Then, Florence Ballard died. It was in February 1976, just a few months after Chudney was born. Florence was only thirty-two years old, but in a way her death was not really a surprise. Her life had been mostly unhappy since she had left the Supremes in 1967. She had gotten married and had had three children. But then her husband had left. Florence had had to go on welfare. She had also started drinking heavily again. She died of alcoholism.

The strongest feeling Diana had about Florence's death was anger. She was angry at herself for not being able to help Florence more. But mostly she was angry at Florence. Florence had quit the Supremes, they hadn't quit her. Florence had been unhappy and had not done anything to change that. Florence had been down and stayed down.

Diana was not going to be like Florence and let her unhappiness eat away at her until it ate her all up. She was not going to be a loser. Diana came to a decision: she was going back to work. She worked so hard that she didn't have time to think about Florence's death. She recorded four albums for release in 1976. She worked up a brand new concert show and went out on the road again.

She and her husband also decided to get divorced. They still loved each other. But they were not happy being married to each other. Diana's husband wanted her home. She wanted to have her career. He didn't like living in her shadow, being known as "Mr. Diana Ross." She could not stay out of the limelight. She wanted to be free. Shortly before their divorce was announced, Bob gave Diana a butterfly pin, saying that butterflies were free, just as she was. "At this point," Diana said at the time, "I don't want to be married to anyone."

Their divorce became final in early 1977. Diana received custody of Rhonda, Tracee, and Chudney, but her ex-husband visited them often. Diana had to face the fact that she had at last failed at something really important: marriage. But she did not wish that she had never tried. She had three beautiful little girls. She could not imagine life without them.

Being newly divorced was easier for Diana than it is for many women. She had money. She had her children and her mother to take care of them. She had her career. And she still had Motown and Berry Gordy. The man and the company had been behind her since she was sixteen years old. Now, at thirty-two, she was glad to have them.

Diana signed a new, seven-year contract with Motown. Then she plunged into her work, recording more albums, starring in a TV special, *An Evening with Diana Ross*, keeping up a heavy schedule of appearances. But she could not keep herself busy enough to forget the pain of her divorce. To make matters worse, her career seemed to go downhill at this time. Motown's new movie, *The Wiz*, a black version of *The Wizard of Oz*, in which she starred, was a flop. Critics said she was too old to play the role of Dorothy and Diana did not like hearing that she was old.

Meanwhile, her latest album, *Ross*, was not doing well. It did not even make the Top 100. For someone like Diana, that was hard to take. She knew what it felt like to have a Number One hit. She did not like being a failure, and that is exactly the way she was feeling about herself at the time.

7

Her Own Boss

Diana was doing a lot of thinking about her life in 1978. The idea occurred to her that maybe she had been living in a dream too long. Maybe she didn't fit into it any more. She had been glamorous Diana Ross of Motown for so long that she had lost track of Diana Ross, person. At the age of thirty-four, she decided to try to look for that Diana Ross.

To do that, she felt she should put some distance between herself and Motown and Berry Gordy. She decided to put a whole continent between them. She moved to New York. She bought an apartment there and sent her daughters to a private school in the city. She did not know New York very well. At first she was afraid and lonely. But after a while she began to feel that it was her home. She was proud of herself for being independent.

In 1979 she recorded a new album called *The Boss*. Even its title seemed to announce to the world that she was more in control of her life. So did some of the songs on the album, like "It's My House" and "I'm in the World." She sang these songs with a stronger voice and a new confidence, too. The album went to the top of the charts. *Diana*, the next album, was even more successful.

Once again, Diana had found a "winning formula" for her records. So, it came as a big surprise to many people when she decided to leave Motown. In 1981 she signed a contract with RCA Records. She had been with Motown for nearly twenty years. Berry Gordy had helped her and guided her for more than half her life. But there were things Diana wanted to do that Gordy and Motown would not allow.

Diana wanted to produce her own albums. She wanted to decide what songs would be on them, what musicians would play the background music, how each song would sound. She wanted to write her own songs and own all the rights to them. She wanted to buy the rights to songs written by others. She could do

none of these things with Motown. Many Motown artists had left the company for the same reason. The Jackson Five had left in 1976 and become the Jacksons because they wanted more creative control. Five years later, Diana left, too. She was grateful to Gordy and Motown for all they had done. But she wanted to be on her own.

Her first album for RCA, *Why Do Fools Fall in Love*, came out that same year, 1981. The next year she did *Silk Electric*. It contained a song called "Muscles" written by Michael Jackson. Diana and Michael co-produced the song, which became a hit single. Her 1983 album for RCA was called *Ross*; in 1984, *Swept Away* was issued. With each new album, she learned more and more about album production.

Diana had full creative control over these records. She also controls every other part of her career, from the publishing of the songs she writes, like "Mirror, Mirror," to the production of her stage acts. She is a one-woman corporation. She has a company to develop new cosmetics and fashion lines. She also has a company to make films, TV specials, and music videos. It is called Anaid (Diana spelled backward).

Diana Ross turned forty in March 1984. But she has never felt so young. Part of being young means feeling as if you can do anything. There are a million things Diana wants to do. Because of all her companies and the control she has over her career, she has the power to do them.

Although most of her business is done in New York, Diana and her daughters and mother live in Connecticut. She wants her children to grow up with lots of grass and trees and away from the centers of the entertainment industry. Her ex-husband, Robert Silberstein, has an apartment nearby, and they are very good friends.

Diana knows she can stand on her own two feet. She is still the feisty little girl from the streets of Detroit. She gets knocked down sometimes. But each time she picks herself up, brushes herself off, and goes back in fighting.

ABOUT THIS BOOK

I started writing books for young people when I was an elementary-school teacher. I wanted my students to read more, and I began to write books about things that they were interested in. They liked to read about people who were famous and how they got to be famous. Most of my students were black, and I wanted them to have books about black people who had overcome poverty and discrimination. These kinds of books were not available when I was growing up in the South. In fact, I could not even use the public library, because I was black.

Although Diana Ross grew up in Detroit, not the South, she had to overcome a lot of barriers because she was poor and black. I have followed her career ever since she began singing with the Supremes. When she played Billie Holiday in *Lady Sings the Blues*, I became even more interested. She was "stretching" her talents. She wasn't content just to be a singer. I feel that she has a lot of courage and has taken many risks in her career.

Many newspaper and magazine articles have been written about Diana Ross. Many of these articles are on microfilm or in large, bound magazine volumes in the library. It was interesting to go through these articles and read what she said years ago. It was fun to look at pictures from twenty years back. Styles in hair and clothing have changed so much. People change, too. The important thing is whether or not they feel good about the changes, whether or not they are able to grow in spirit. Diana Ross has.   J.H.